RANGER in TIME

Journey through Ash and Smoke

THE RANGER IN TIME SERIES

RANGER in TIME

Journey through Ash and Smoke

KATE MESSNER

illustrated by
KELLEY McMORRIS

Scholastic Inc.

Text copyright © 2017 by Kate Messner
Illustrations by Kelley McMorris, copyright © 2017 Scholastic Inc.

This book is being published simultaneously in hardcover by Scholastic Press.

All rights reserved. Published by Scholastic Inc., *Publishers since 1920.* SCHOLASTIC, SCHOLASTIC PRESS, and associated logos are trademarks and/or registered trademarks of Scholastic Inc.

The publisher does not have any control over and does not assume any responsibility for author or third-party websites or their content.

No part of this publication may be reproduced, stored in a retrieval system, or transmitted in any form or by any means, electronic, mechanical, photocopying, recording, or otherwise, without written permission of the publisher. For information regarding permission, write to Scholastic Inc., Attention: Permissions Department, 557 Broadway, New York, NY 10012.

While inspired by real events and historical characters, this is a work of fiction and does not claim to be historically accurate or portray factual events or relationships. Please keep in mind that references to actual persons, living or dead, business establishments, events, or locales may not be factually accurate, but rather fictionalized by the author.

Library of Congress Cataloging-in-Publication Data
Names: Messner, Kate, author. | McMorris, Kelley, illustrator. | Messner, Kate. Ranger in time.
Title: Journey through ash and smoke / Kate Messner ; illustrated by Kelley McMorris.
Description: New York, NY : Scholastic Inc., [2017] | Series: Ranger in time | Summary: Ranger, the time-traveling golden retriever, has landed in Viking age Iceland, where he meets a girl named Helga, who seems perfectly able to take care of herself — until an erupting volcano and an early arriving baby force Ranger and Helga to journey through the ash and smoke to find her father and bring him home.
Identifiers: LCCN 2016011672
Subjects: LCSH: Golden retriever — Juvenile fiction. | Time travel — Juvenile fiction. | Volcanoes — Juvenile fiction. | Adventure stories. | Iceland — History — To 1262 — Juvenile fiction. | CYAC: Golden retriever — Fiction. | Dogs — Fiction. | Time travel — Fiction. | Volcanoes — Fiction. | Adventure and adventurers — Fiction. | Iceland — History — To 1262 — Fiction. | GSAFD: Adventure fiction.
Classification: LCC PZ10.3.M5635 Lan 2017 | DDC 813.6 — dc23
LC record available at http://lccn.loc.gov/2016011672

ISBN 978-0-545-90978-5

10 9 8 7   19 20 21

Printed in the United States of America   40
First printing 2017

Book design by Ellen Duda

*For Melissa Guerrette
and her amazing OES readers*

Chapter 1

RUNAWAY HORSE!

Rain blew sideways as Helga hurried home with a basket full of eiderdown from the lakeshore. The nests of the plump black-and-white birds were lined with soft feathers in early summer. Those feathers were used for bedding, and Helga had collected more than usual today. Father would be pleased. The down would sell for a good amount of silver on his next trading voyage.

Helga huddled over the basket as she walked, protecting the feathers from the wind and rain. The turf roof of her family's longhouse had just appeared in the distance when the ground rumbled under her sheep-skin shoes.

It wasn't the first time she'd felt this since her family's ship arrived.

They'd left Norway as the snow was melting, in a boat loaded with sheep, goats, horses, and grain. They'd packed fishing line, nets, and hooks so they could eat until the barley grew. Helga had climbed onto the boat with her mother and father, a farmhand named Gunnarr, and Asa, the weaver woman. Helga was an only child, but her mother's belly was fat with a baby that would arrive soon. Helga knew her father hoped for a boy, to help with the new farm.

Two other families had piled onto the boat with Helga's, and they'd set off to sea. Helga remembered the sound of the sail, flapping and snapping in the wind as their ship cut through the frigid ocean. Father had read the sun and stars to find their way. After seven days of pounding, icy waves, Iceland's jagged cliffs and ice-capped mountains had appeared in the distance. Their ship had landed in the calm harbor near the farm where her father's brother lived with his family.

Helga knew she would never forget her first look at this new land. The plumes of smoke that rose from the earth were like nothing she had seen at home. Not only did the earth here bubble and send up steam, it trembled from time to time as well.

This morning, the shaking was stronger than usual. Helga flopped her dress over her basket, hugged it to her chest, and ran the rest of the way home.

When she reached the longhouse, she pushed open the heavy, wooden door and stepped inside. The rock weight that hung from the doorframe dropped to pull the door closed behind her. New sounds replaced the drumming of the rain. Restless sheep bleated in the stalls. Asa hummed at her loom. Stew bubbled as Mother stirred a pot over the fire at the center of the hall.

"Where is Father?" Helga asked. She pulled off her kerchief and placed it on a bench alongside the basket of down.

"Out chasing Rosta. That horse spooks so easily." Mother shook her head. "Your father had gone to see Ingar Olaffson about their property argument. But then the trembling began and the horse took off running."

"I will go help Father search." Helga was good with the old horse and liked to remind her father that she was a hard worker. She could do any job a son could do, and get it done long before the new baby grew old enough to be useful. So she tightened her cloak and started back out into the wind and rain.

She crossed the barley fields and wandered the shoreline. She climbed the gravel ridge that separated the lake from the sea and scanned the land in the distance.

But Helga could see neither her father nor his horse. She walked farther, to the vast fields of black rock and darkened tunnels. Perhaps Rosta was hiding in one of the larger caves.

The rain grew heavier. Helga wished she hadn't left her kerchief at home. Jagged rocks poked through her shoes and scratched the bottoms of her feet with every step.

"Rosta!" Helga slapped her hands on her knees. She made kiss sounds with her mouth, like she did when she brought the old horse food. But there was no sign of Rosta, and now rain poured from the sky.

Helga skipped from rock to rock over a rushing creek, slipping and sliding on the wet stones. "Father! Rosta!" she shouted. But the rain swallowed her words. She'd never hear Father, even if he called back to her.

Helga ducked under a stony bridge that spanned an area of soggy grass and ferns. Beyond that was a rocky tunnel. Helga crouched low and crawled into the sheltered dark to catch her breath.

The streams that flowed from the mountains were already rushing from the rain. Helga knew even from her short time in this land that too much water could sweep a person away. She would have to turn back. She hoped Father had found Rosta and was already on his way home.

Helga shook off her cloak, took a deep breath, and climbed back out into the blowing rain. She turned to where she thought the longhouse must be, but the clouds were so thick and low she couldn't see past the rocks in front of her. Helga turned, but the view was the same in every direction — walls of cloud and water, coming down faster than ever. Was her family's longhouse before her or behind her?

The water puddled under Helga's feet. She splashed forward but had no idea if she was headed for home. She couldn't see the stream that cut through a wide crevice in the rocks nearby, but she could hear it roaring.

"Father! Rosta!" she called.

But only the wind answered.

Chapter 2

THE NEW PUPPY

"Come on, Ranger!" Luke called as he ran through the backyard toward the driveway. "Let's meet Zeeshan's new puppy!"

The Tarar family's van had just pulled in. Luke and Sadie's friends Zeeshan and Noreen jumped out of the backseat. They waved to their parents as the van pulled away.

"Hey, guys!" Zeeshan turned to Luke and Sadie and held up a fluffy, brown fur ball. Skinny legs with oversize paws poked out from the fuzz. "This is Muggsy! Isn't she cute?"

Luke and Sadie ran up to the fur ball and started petting and kissing it. Ranger stayed back and waited for his hugs and ear scratches from Zeeshan and Noreen. He waited a long time. Then he barked.

"Oh! Hiya, Ranger!" Noreen turned away from the fur ball and gave him a pat on the head. "Did you see our new puppy?"

Ranger stepped up to Zeeshan and sniffed the fur ball. It smelled doggy and new. Soapy, too. Ranger sneezed, and everyone laughed.

"Let's go show Mom and Dad." Luke led everyone to the front door and held it open. "You coming, Ranger, or do you want to stay outside a while?"

Ranger barked and turned back to the yard. If everyone was going to snuggle the fur ball, he'd rather dig or chase squirrels.

Ranger sniffed at the edge of Mom's garden. He dug in the wet mud a while, but there

was nothing interesting today, so he flopped down in the grass and let the sun warm his muddy fur. He was about to fall asleep when a different kind of fur ball zipped past him across the lawn.

Squirrel!

Ranger jumped to his feet and raced after it. He chased the squirrel through Mom's vegetable garden, out to the driveway and back again, and twice around the picnic table. Finally, the squirrel leaped onto a tree and scratched its way up to a high branch.

Ranger had never actually caught a squirrel, even though he loved chasing them. That was why he couldn't be an official search-and-rescue dog. Ranger had gone through special training with Luke and Dad, learning how to track scents and find missing people. But in order to be a search-and-rescue dog, you had to ignore the squirrels that zipped past during your test session. Ranger hadn't quite man-aged that. If a real live person needed help, he wouldn't chase squirrels. He would help. But on the day of the test, Ranger knew that Luke was only pretending to be lost. And that squir-rel's tail had been especially fluffy.

Just like the squirrel in the tree, chattering down at him now. Ranger was tired of being scolded. He trotted to the porch and went in through his dog door to get a drink of water.

"Whoa, Ranger!" Luke said as he walked past. "You're all muddy. I better start a bath. Stay here so Mom doesn't freak out, okay?"

Ranger whined when he heard water run-ning upstairs. He didn't like baths. He enjoyed the warm water once he was in, but the tub was hard and slippery under his paws, and when he got out he always smelled funny. Like that too-clean fur ball. Like flowers and apples instead of mud and dog.

"Come on up, Ranger!" Luke called.

Ranger started for the back stairs, but a humming sound from his dog bed made him stop.

Ranger turned and pawed at his blanket until it fell aside to reveal the old first aid kit he'd dug up from the garden on a different day. The worn metal box was humming more loudly now. It was a sound Ranger knew — one that he heard only when someone far away needed help.

Once, when Ranger had heard the sound, he'd gone to help a boy named Sam whose family was on a dangerous journey. Another time, he'd rescued a boy named Marcus in a big arena with fighting and wild animals. He'd walked many miles with a girl named Sarah and her brother, Jesse, as they searched for safety and freedom. And he'd shivered in the cold with a boy named Jack who dreamed of being an explorer.

All those times, Ranger had been able to help the children. He'd done his job and come home to Luke with treasures tucked under his collar — a quilt square, a funny leaf, a feather, and a tattered picture etched in charcoal. Those things were all nestled in Ranger's dog bed or on the wall nearby.

Now the box was humming again.

Ranger nuzzled the leather strap of the old first aid kit until it looped over his head. Ranger felt the metal box grow warm, then hot at his throat.

Luke might have been calling him for his bath, but all Ranger could hear was the high-pitched humming, growing louder and louder. Light spilled from the cracks in the box, flooding the mudroom with brightness.

Ranger felt as if he were being squeezed through a hole in the sky. The light grew so bright, he had to close his eyes.

When he opened them, the humming had stopped, and the bright light was gone. Fire flickered in a shadowy room. Wind whistled through cracks in the walls. The air smelled of rain and salt, people and animals, and sharp, earthy smoke.

"Helga!" a woman's voice called. Ranger turned and saw her, leaning out the open door of a long, narrow building with walls made of stone and dirt. "Helga!" she screamed into the storm outside. Her voice was full of fear.

Ranger didn't know where he was or who Helga was, but he understood one thing as the wind whipped rain in through the door: This was no day to be outside.

Chapter 3

LOST IN THE LAVA

Ranger barked, and the woman turned to face him. Her dress was longer than the ones Luke and Sadie's mother wore. Her silver hair was woven into a braid. Her face was full of worry, and she held a wet cloth, like a scarf, twisting it between her hands.

The woman frowned at Ranger. Then she turned and shouted into the rain again. "Helga!"

Ranger trotted up to her and sniffed the scarf thing. It smelled like a person but not

17

the woman. A different person. Maybe the Helga person the woman was calling.

Ranger knew he'd have work to do before he left this place of blowing rain. Maybe he could find the Helga person. Ranger sniffed the scarf again and squeezed past the woman out the door.

The ground was soggy and sandy under Ranger's paws. The wind whipped rain into his ears, but Ranger ignored that and sniffed the cool air. The only scents he caught were wet rock, mud, and rain.

Ranger had gone through weeks of search-and-rescue training at home with Dad and Luke. He'd practiced tracking Luke on breezy, sunny days and on gusty, stormy days. Those were toughest. Damp weather was fine. But heavy rain could wash away a scent, and wind scattered what was left of it. Today was one of those days.

Ranger circled back, over and over. His fur was soaked and cold. He walked along a lakeshore, sniffing the air, hoping for a scent of the scarf thing and the Helga person.

Just beyond the lake, the land changed from flat and sandy to rough, with jagged black rocks that scratched Ranger's paws. But he kept going, lifting his nose to sniff the wild, wet air.

Nothing.

Finally, Ranger went down a hill and squeezed between two big rocks that blocked the wind. It felt good not to have raindrops pelting his nose. Ranger paused but knew he couldn't rest for long. He had to keep searching. Just as he was about to go back into the open wind . . .

There!

Mixed with the wind and rain in this sheltered spot, he caught the scent of the Helga person.

Slowly, Ranger stepped out from the rocks. He sniffed until he caught the scent again.

The rain was a little lighter now. That helped. Ranger followed the scent through the ragged landscape. One of his paws was scratched and bleeding, but now that he had the scent, he wasn't going to lose it. He tracked it to a dark, open space, crept to the edge, and sniffed.

"Rosta?" someone said from the dark.

It was the Helga person from the scarf! Her scent filled the cave. Ranger barked.

Helga gasped. Then she crawled out and sighed. "You are not who I was hoping to see, dog."

The girl was about as tall as Luke, but she looked stronger. She had thick arms, broad shoulders, and a dripping braid down her back. She wore a long dress and over that, an apron thing. Its straps were fastened together by a chain and two shiny, round disks of metal.

The Helga girl held out her hand. Ranger sniffed it. She smelled like sweat, mud, rocks, and bird.

Thunder boomed in the sky, and rain burst from the clouds again. Ranger whined. He hated thunder, even when he could hide in his dog bed or snuggle with Luke and Sadie.

Ranger didn't like this soggy cave, either, but he climbed down to the girl and nudged her toward the opening.

Helga pushed back. "We can't go out now," she said. "Not in this storm."

The thunder boomed again. Then came another sound, long and rushing and deep. Ranger pricked up his ears and rushed to the opening of the cave.

"What is it, dog?" Helga asked. She followed him and crawled up to look. "Oh no! The creek's flooding!"

Chapter 4

SWEPT AWAY

Water poured into the cave as Helga climbed out. The creek that usually wandered through the nearby hills in a gentle cascade spilled over its banks, streaming toward them in a frothy rush.

Helga sucked in her breath. She had seen storms like this before. Soon, the whole low area would be flooded. She needed to get home. But which way was home?

Ranger's paws slipped on the wet rock as he climbed up beside her. Helga put a hand on his matted head and looked down at him with bright, scared eyes.

The skin on Ranger's neck prickled. The smell of the air was changing by the second. It was wetter, strong with the scent of crumbling rocks and plants torn up by the waves of water raging down the hills. Helga needed shelter, and Ranger knew where that was — back at the stone-and-dirt building, with the woman who had called for her.

Ranger trotted away from Helga and circled, sniffing the air and rocks until he picked up the path he'd taken to find her.

There!

Ranger caught his own scent and recognized the smell of some mossy plants near the sharp rocks. This was the way he'd come before. He barked and ran a few steps along the scent trail. But Helga didn't follow.

Ranger splashed back and jumped up on Helga with his paws, pushing her in the right direction. Helga stumbled and looked down at him. Water swirled around her ankles. Ranger barked and started tracking the old scent trail again.

Finally, Helga followed him through the rocks.

It was slippery. Ranger did his best to plant his paws as he crossed the creek. He braced himself against rushing water that threatened to sweep him away.

As Ranger was climbing out of the water between two pointed rocks, Helga slipped and fell backward. She flailed at the rocks but couldn't hold on. The water swept her along as if she weighed no more than one of Sadie's dolls.

Ranger jumped into the churning flood.

The water was too strong. He couldn't keep his paws on the creek bottom, so he paddled against the current, struggling to keep his head above water. Where was the Helga girl?

The raging water slammed Helga into a cluster of rocks. She cried out in pain, but when her feet found solid ground, she was strangely thankful for the sharp rock that had gouged her cheek. Without it, the flood might have washed her clear out to sea.

Helga clung to the rock and scrambled to stand. She caught a glimpse of the golden dog, paddling against the current. She held tightly to a corner of rock with one hand. With the other, she reached out and grabbed a thick handful of wet fur.

Ranger yelped.

"I'm sorry!" the girl said. She pulled Ranger

to her, let go of his fur, and gripped the collar around his neck. "I didn't want you to be carried off!"

With water still swirling around her knees, Helga took a careful step. She kept one hand on the rocks and the other on Ranger's collar. She pushed through the water, rock to rock to rock, in what she hoped was the direction of home.

Ranger looked up at the girl. She had a cut below one eye. Blood trickled down her cheek, but she hardly seemed to notice. She started out going the right way, so Ranger went along when she pulled him gently by his collar. But then she tugged him off to the left.

That wasn't where he'd come from. Ranger tugged back and barked. Helga stopped and looked down at him. Then she looked around and set off in his direction.

Soon, the rain eased and the water slowed.

They sloshed through puddles until Helga spotted the lake with its familiar shoreline. She let go of the dog and started to run.

Ranger was happy to be out of the deep, fast water. He splashed alongside Helga, all the way back to the strange, earthy house. The woman was outside, still holding the scarf thing. Now there was a man, too, standing beside a brown-and-white horse.

"Father!" Helga shouted as she raced up to him. "You found Rosta!"

"Never mind Rosta," he said. "I'm thankful to have found you." He looked down at Ranger. "What's this?"

"This dog is the one who found me," she said, scratching Ranger behind his ear. He tipped his head and leaned into her strong hand. "I took shelter in one of the caves, and —" Helga stopped talking when she noticed blood on her father's hands. "Are you hurt?"

"What?" Her father seemed confused. Then he looked down at his palms. "Oh! No. I had to kill a fox that was after the hens. I must go take care of the meat." He looked at Helga's mud-soaked dress. "And you'd better clean yourself up before our evening meal."

"Yes, Father." Helga's parents went inside the longhouse, but she stayed outside. She patted Ranger on his matted fur and let her hand rest on the metal box he wore around his neck. She hadn't seen it before, in the chaos of the storm. "What's that you have?" She eased the box from around Ranger's neck and fiddled with the clasps until it opened. "Bandages and things." She looked at Ranger and said, "I'll put this inside."

Ranger followed Helga into the longhouse, where she tucked Ranger's first aid kit under one of the sleeping benches. Then she knelt down so she and Ranger were nose to soggy nose. "Thank you for helping me find my way home," Helga said. "You can have some food and sleep by my bench tonight if you'd like. But first . . ." She sniffed his wet fur. "You must have a bath."

Chapter 5

BATH TIME

The hot spring wasn't far away — just up into the hills a bit. Now that the rain had stopped, it wasn't a bad walk, but Helga was still cold. She led Ranger along the well-worn path until she saw steam rising against the dark hills.

Ranger sniffed the misty air. Amid the mud and plants, he caught the old scent trails of many people and animals who had come this way. There was another smell, too — a hot, sour scent, like when Luke and Sadie's mom boiled eggs too long on the stove.

"Look!" Helga said as they crested a hill. A girl about Helga's age and two younger boys sat in a steaming pool of water nestled in the boulders below. "Thora and Ozurr and Bersi are here. They're my cousins." Helga waved and raced down the hill with Ranger at her side.

"Whose shaggy hound is that?" Ozurr asked as Helga sat down on a flat rock.

"I'm not certain," Helga said. She pulled off her dripping shoes and wiggled her toes. "But he seems to have adopted me, and we are both in need of a bath."

"You look as if you've had a horrible start to the day," Thora said, skimming her hand over the surface of the hot water.

"We went searching for Rosta after he ran off this morning," Helga said as she changed out of her rain-soaked dress and spread it over a bush near the pool. "We were out in the storm and got caught in a swollen creek."

"You're lucky," Bersi said, bobbing in the warm water. "Father says it's easy to be swept away when it rains so much."

"He's right. But I'm safe now. Just a bit chilled." Helga looked up as the sun peeked through the clouds. She hoped her things would dry before she had to put them back on.

She dipped a foot into the steaming water, then eased herself the rest of the way in, sat down, and leaned back against a mossy rock. She breathed in the humid air, closed her eyes, and let the water warm her from the outside in.

"Did you find your horse?" Thora asked.

"We did," Helga said. While she told Thora the rest of the story, Ranger stepped up to the edge of the hot, rocky pool. It was the strangest little pond he'd ever seen. Ranger played around the lake at the park with Luke some-times, but that water was cold and fresh and weedy. This water seemed more like a bath, but with that odd, eggy smell and a rocky, sandy bottom. At least his paws wouldn't slide all over like they did in the tub at home. Ranger crouched and poked one foot into the hot water. It stung the paw that he'd scratched on the rocks earlier. Ranger pulled his foot back and whined.

Helga opened her eyes. "It's all right, dog," she said. "The water's nice and warm." She splashed a little water at Ranger. Thora's little brothers began splashing, too. Ranger backed away. "Leave him be," Helga said. "He'll decide when to come in."

Ranger remembered how good the warm bathwater felt at home, once he was in. He dipped his paw in the water and leaned for-ward, just a bit.

Then he slipped on a rock and slid into the pool with an enormous splash.

Helga and her cousins laughed. "I suppose that's fair, dog," Helga said, wiping water from her face. "We did splash you first."

Ranger sloshed over beside her and sat down. The water was hot, but not too hot to feel good. Helga had just started scratching behind his ear when something rustled in the bushes.

Ranger's ears pricked up. He sat taller, sniffed the air, and caught a doggy smell that wasn't his own.

"What's that?" Helga said, leaning over to look.

"A mouse in the bushes?" said one of the boys.

"It's too big for a mouse," Thora said.

The bush rustled again. Then a small, black nose poked out.

"Oh!" Helga glided through the water to the edge of the pool and reached her hand toward the nose. She made quiet clicking noises with her tongue. "Come on out. It's all right."

The nose poked out some more, and behind it came a tiny fur ball that reminded Ranger of Zeeshan and Noreen's new puppy.

"It's a fox pup!" Helga whispered as it crept to the edge of the pool and sniffed her fingers. The pup was fluffy gray and white, with ears and paws too big for the rest of its body. Its curious green-gold eyes darted from the children to Ranger and back again.

The pup left Helga and circled the pool, sniffing each child's hand and all the rocky edges and patches of sand. When an insect fluttered in a patch of grass, the fox pup crouched low, pawing the ground.

It was still for a moment. Then its leg muscles twitched . . . and it pounced!

But the pup misjudged and soared right over whatever bug was in the grass. It landed on crumbly, loose rocks at the edge of the pool and skidded into the water.

Splash!

Helga and her cousins laughed, but Ranger sensed the pup's panic as it kicked in the hot water. Ranger sloshed across the pool, lowered his nose, and nudged the little fox back onto land. The pup shook itself, spraying Ranger and everything else. Then it rolled in the dirt a few times and pounced back into the pool.

This time, Ranger left it in the water and let it kick. It turned out the little fox could swim just fine.

The pup paddled over to Helga, who scooped it up, kissed its nose, and said, "Where's your mother, little one?" Then her face fell. "Oh no!"

"What's wrong?" Thora asked.

"Father said this morning that he had to kill a fox that was after the hens." Helga's heart sank. "I fear it was this pup's mother."

While Thora helped her brothers get dressed, Helga set the fox pup down on shore. It stayed close to her while she put on her clothes, sniffing and pawing at the rocks. When Helga sat to put her shoes on, the fox stretched out beside her and yawned.

Ranger climbed out of the hot pool, shook himself off, and lay down by a rock. The sun was finally out, and it felt good.

Helga wandered all around the bushes and rocks near the hot pool with the fox pup prancing at her heels. Finally, she scooped the little fox up in her arms and sighed. "I'm so sorry," she whispered, hugging it close to her damp dress. "There's no sign of your mother here. But you can come home with us." She looked over at Ranger and added, "You'll have a friend to play with."

Helga put the pup down. It trotted over to Ranger and pounced on his front paw. Ranger moved his paw out of the way, and the pup pounced again. Then it licked Ranger's nose.

"I don't think your father will be pleased," Thora said.

"Father is the reason the pup needs our help," Helga said. "But I'm sure you're right." She looked down at the tiny fox and sighed. "We'll have to keep you a secret for now," Helga said. "Father doesn't care for foxes."

Thora and her brothers started toward their own longhouse over the hills. "Shall we hunt eggs at the cliffs tomorrow?" Thora called back to Helga.

"Yes," Helga said. "We can meet there when the sun comes up." She looked down at Ranger and the tiny fox. "Let's go home, friends."

The pup raced in a circle around Ranger, swiped at his tail a few times, and trotted off after Helga.

Ranger didn't think he cared for foxes, either. He ignored the pup and walked beside Helga, heading for the earthen house with the smoke curling up from the roof. Hopefully, he'd be able to finish his work here soon and go home.

Chapter 6

TINY TROUBLE

Delicious smells drifted out of the longhouse when they returned and Helga pulled open the door. Roasting meat and warm, earthy plant scents. Ranger lifted his nose and breathed it in.

But deep, sharp voices spilled out the door along with the wonderful smells. Helga caught a glimpse of Ingar Olaffson and guessed he'd come to argue about the farm boundaries again. Father would be in a sour mood all night.

Helga draped her cloak over the fox pup she carried, stepped back, and pulled Ranger by his collar until the door swung shut and they were all outside again.

"Father has a visitor, and it does not seem to be going well," Helga whispered to Ranger. She crouched behind the rubbish pile, and pulled him by the collar to join her. "We'll have to wait here."

Ranger sat down and waited with Helga. He didn't understand what she was saying to him, but he understood that sometimes, people just needed to talk. Luke did that, most often when he was worried or scared. Helga seemed that way now. Ranger could feel her heart pounding through her dress.

The fox pup tried to wiggle away from Helga, but she held it tight. "What shall we call you, little one?" she said. "How about Funi? I think that suits you well." *Funi* was the word for fire, and this pup's eyes always held a spark or two.

Finally, the longhouse door opened. Ingar Olaffson stormed out, stomped to his horse, and rode away with a scowl on his face. Helga's father was upset, too. His loud voice carried through the turf walls as he spoke to her mother.

Helga waited until it was quiet. Then she arranged some rocks and bones from the rubbish pile to make a small shelter for the fox pup. "You'll have to stay here for now, Funi," she said, and turned for the door.

Funi jumped up onto the rocks, tumbled over the wobbly fence Helga had built, and pounced on her shoe.

Helga sighed, put the pup back, and piled the wall higher. Then she turned to Ranger and pointed to the ground near the pup's homemade cage. "Wait here. I'll be back, I

promise." She pointed again, and Ranger sat down.

He stood guard while Helga went inside. Funi got up on his hind legs and tried to climb out. Ranger gently pawed him back down.

Funi yipped. Ranger sat with his back to the pup, blocking the way out of the little pen.

The fox pup climbed up and swiped at Ranger with a paw. Tiny claws scratched Ranger's back, but he stayed put. If this was the job he had to do to go home to Luke, he'd do it. But Ranger hoped he'd be done soon.

Finally, Helga came back carrying two stew-covered bones. She gave the big one to Ranger and dropped the smaller one into Funi's pen. The pup pounced on the bone and lapped up the greasy stew that covered it.

Ranger lay down with his bone between his paws and began chewing on one end. Helga tucked her dress around her legs and sat beside him, patting his head. "You'll need to stay here tonight," she said, "but tomorrow, Father is leaving, so you'll be able to come inside. And then . . ." She wasn't sure what would happen then.

Father had been packing when she went inside the longhouse. He was leaving in the morning for Thingvellir — where the island people gathered to make laws and settle disputes like the one her father and Ingar Olaffson were having over the borders of their barley fields.

Helga had never been to Thingvellir, but she'd heard stories from their local chieftain. He joined the island's other leaders there for the Althing, a two-week assembly each summer. There, the Law Speaker would read the island's laws from a tall cliff called the Law Rock. Announcements were made about property and other issues that affected the whole island.

Anyone with a problem could bring it to the Althing to be settled.

Helga always wondered what the Althing would be like when she watched their chieftain ride off each summer. Women were allowed to be chieftains but had to nominate a man to represent them at the Althing. Mother always said that's because women had to stay home to run the farms; men couldn't be trusted to do that for two weeks alone with their wives away.

Now, Mother and Helga would need to take care of the farm, with help from Asa and Gunnarr. Mother's belly was very fat with the baby now, so Helga knew she would need to take on extra work. She didn't mind. She only hoped Father's property argument would be settled, and he would be happy again when he returned.

"Helga!" her mother called.

"I am taking care of the rubbish and will be right there!" Helga shouted back. She turned to Ranger and Funi and pointed to the ground. "Stay here. I'll be back with breakfast for you in the morning." And she ran into the house.

Funi whined and started climbing over the fence, pawing at Ranger's shoulder. Ranger gently pushed the pup down and watched the longhouse door swing shut.

Funi yipped again and swatted Ranger's tail.

It was going to be a very long night.

Chapter 7

THE CLIFF OVER THE SEA

Father set out at dawn the next morning on his brother's horse, leaving Rosta for Helga and Gunnarr to use while he was gone. Helga waved into the pink light until she couldn't see her father anymore.

Then she hurried out to the rubbish pile. She knelt down beside Ranger with a handful of dried fish. "I've brought you some breakfast."

Ranger sniffed. It was very fishy. But he was very hungry, so he gobbled it up. Funi ate his, too, and then pawed at his fence.

Helga leaned over and lifted him out. The pup celebrated his freedom by racing around the longhouse twice, stopping to bat at Ranger's tail for a while, and racing around again.

Helga laughed. "I see you're happy to be out, but we have a lot of work to do with Father away. You can both come with me to the cliffs to gather puffin eggs with Thora."

The sky was a perfect blue as they started out on the path. Helga led Ranger and Funi through the rocky area where she'd gone searching for Rosta the day before. In the sunshine, it was hard to imagine how she'd gotten so lost, but when the weather changed here, it happened fast and fierce.

Ranger stayed close to Helga, but Funi raced around the rocks. He scampered over a craggy bridge, slid down into a shadowy tunnel, and popped up through a mossy opening farther along.

"He wants us to chase him!" Helga said, laughing.

Ranger didn't want to chase anybody. He wanted to do his work so he could go home.

But Helga took off running, and Ranger followed her. His paw was still tender from the scratches he got the day before, so he tried to avoid the sharp rocks by staying on the damp, mossy areas.

Ranger padded down a small hill onto one of those deep-green patches. The moss felt cool and soft under his paws. But suddenly, the ground collapsed underneath him. Ranger landed in a dark, rocky place a few feet below and yelped.

"Oh! Are you all right, dog?" Helga peered down at him. Ranger wasn't hurt badly, but he'd landed hard, and his paws stung again. He barked up at her.

"You must have stepped where the moss was covering a hole. You have to watch out for that. Here . . ." Helga lay down on her belly and reached down into the darkness. "Come on . . . jump up! Up!"

Ranger wasn't sure if he could jump high enough to get out of the hole, but before he could try, Helga slid down, wrapped her arms around his middle, and hoisted him up onto solid ground. Then she found a foothold in the rocks, and climbed out herself.

She brushed the mud from her hands. "Ready to go now?"

Ranger kept to the bare rocks after that. His paws were sore, but he didn't trust the moss anymore. Helga reached down and scratched his head as they walked. Ranger leaned into her hand, but he didn't feel quite

right about it. He was supposed to have rescued Helga. Not the other way around.

As they approached the seaside cliffs, Helga spotted her favorite flowers: purple, white, and yellow blossoms that grew right out of the stones.

When they'd first arrived, Helga wondered how anything could grow in such a stark, windblown place. But Mother had told her that when a seed settles to earth, if it's tough, it can make the rockiest shore into home. Mother promised that Helga, too, could grow where she had landed.

Helga had tried to do that, working to help her family and learning to call this new land home. But she missed her family and neighbors back in Norway. At least Thora was here. But she was so busy caring for her younger brothers that she rarely had time to spend with Helga.

At least they could collect eggs together, and it was a perfect day for that. The path to the cliffs was muddy, but otherwise, there was no sign of the wild weather from the day before. There were no more threatening clouds — only a few bright puffs of white. One reminded Helga of a horse, but with extra legs trailing into the blue.

"Look!" She pointed and traced its outline with her finger. "Perhaps that is Sleipnir in the sky."

Father had told her about Sleipnir, the eight-legged horse ridden by Odin, the god of wisdom and war. Odin ruled Valhalla, where warriors went if they died a brave death. Helga's grandfather had been killed in battle before she was born. He'd gone off with the valkyries, Father said. They were warrior women who searched battlefields for dead heroes and carried them to Valhalla.

Helga liked imagining her grandfather there with Odin, drinking mead and eating fattened pigs. But she still wished she could have had time with him here, in this world. She couldn't help feeling jealous of Odin and his strange-looking horse in the sky.

By the time Helga looked away from the clouds, they'd almost reached the top of the cliffs. Waves pounded the smooth, round stones below. Sometimes, Helga and Thora scrambled down the rocky path to fish from the beach, but today, they would hunt from above.

Helga looked down the path toward the lake. There was no sign of Thora yet, but she could start on her own. Helga pulled a long coil of walrus-skin rope from her woolen bag and turned toward the cliff. Funi leaped at the rope and grabbed it with both front paws. Helga was so surprised she dropped it, and Funi wrestled it in the dirt as if it were alive.

"Nice hunting!" Helga laughed. She took the rope and held it out of Funi's reach. "I'm sorry, but I need this. You'll have to play with something else."

Funi went back to swatting Ranger's tail, while Helga tied one end of the rope around a strong rocky crag near the top of the cliff. She looped the other end around her waist, tied it into a knot, and pulled it tight. Then she walked to the edge of the cliff and peered over. The puffins were active, flying in and out of their nests in the craggy rocks, bringing fish to their partners. It would be a good day to collect eggs. Helga leaned a little farther over the edge for a better look.

Ranger pawed at the muddy ground and whined. She was making him nervous, so close to the edge like that. Sometimes, Luke and Sadie's family had picnics at a park with a stream and high waterfall. Their mom never let them get close to the edge like this. Ranger wished she were here now to make Helga come back to where it was safer.

But Ranger was on his own. He barked and pawed the ground again.

Helga looked back at him. "It's all right, dog," she said. "I'm good at egg hunting." Then she stepped over the edge of the cliff and disappeared.

Chapter 8

PUFFINS AND PLAY

Ranger barked. Carefully, he inched his way to the top of the cliff and looked over. There was Helga, holding the rope around her waist with one hand, reaching into a crevice with the other. Fat black-and-white birds flew all around her, darting in and out of their nests.

Helga pulled a cream-colored egg from an empty nest and held it up. Then she tucked it into the bag strapped to her side, pushed off the rocks with her feet, and swung herself over to another spot along the cliff.

Soon, Thora came hurrying down the path. She walked right to the edge of the cliff and called down to Helga, "Good hunting today?"

"Very good!" Helga plucked another egg from a nest and tucked it into her bag. "Come down!" She pushed off the rocks with her legs and swung to another spot, while Thora tied her own rope and lowered herself to join her cousin.

Ranger watched them dangling and swinging for a few minutes. Then he stepped back from the edge. Helga and Thora seemed fine, but watching them down there was making his neck feel all prickly. He turned away from the sea and went to sniff at some other rocks. They smelled like mice or voles might live under them.

Mice, Ranger decided. But different from the home mice that snuck into the mudroom when the weather got cold in the fall. Ranger sniffed again and heard a frightened yelp behind him.

Funi was pawing frantically at the ground, scratching and clawing at the loose rocks and mud while his hind legs dangled over the edge of the cliff.

Ranger raced back. The earth here was unstable. Ranger felt the rocks and dirt shifting, but there was no time to find careful footing. He lunged forward, grabbed the scruff of Funi's neck in his teeth, and yanked the pup back onto the ledge.

Funi yipped at Ranger and shook himself. Ranger stepped between Funi and the edge and nudged the pup away from the cliff. Then Ranger sat down, keeping watch. Every time Funi started to stand up, a big golden paw pushed him down again.

It wasn't long before Helga's head appeared over the edge of the cliff. She hoisted herself up on the rope, untied it from the rocks, and began to coil it around her arm. Funi jumped up, raced to her side, and swiped at the end of the rope with a paw.

"Have you been waiting for us?" Helga laughed. She dangled her rope and swung it back and forth as she waited for Thora to climb up, too. Funi leaped and pounced and batted and swatted until he was all tired out.

The girls coiled their ropes and tucked them in the woolen sacks.

"Not a bad day at all," Thora said, patting her lumpy bag.

Helga reached into her own bag and pulled out a smooth, white egg. She cracked it on a rock, tipped her head back, and poured the gooey insides into her mouth. Then she knelt by a smooth-topped rock with a little indentation and said, "Here . . ." She cracked another egg and spilled its contents onto the rock.

Funi started lapping it up, but Helga pulled him back a bit. "You have to share."

Ranger stepped up to the rock and licked at the egg stuff. He had bites of Luke's eggs on Sunday mornings sometimes. This was different. Cold and runny, but still good.

When Ranger and Funi had finished their egg, Helga and Thora started down the path to the beach. The girls descended the rugged cliff quickly, as if it were just a few easy stairs. Funi zipped ahead of them, pouncing from rock to rock.

Ranger went more slowly. He was heavier, and some of the stones crumbled and shifted as he eased down the bank. He didn't like walking on earth that moved under his paws, but he took his time, and soon he jumped down onto the beach.

Helga picked up a smooth, round stone and tossed it into the shallow waves. Funi raced after it, and Ranger did, too. The water was cold, but it felt good.

Helga and Thora carefully laid down their sacks of eggs, took off their shoes, and waded in, too. They splashed in the foamy water as the tide came in. Funi pranced alongside them until a wave swept his paws out from under him. The little fox scampered to the beach and shook the salty spray from his fur.

The swells were growing bigger. Each wave seemed to break a little stronger than the last. Ranger barked and backed up onto the wet rocks. He didn't like the way the current was tugging at him. He wanted the girls to come out where it was shallower. Where it was safe.

Ranger barked again.

Thora turned to look at him. "What is it, dog? Don't you like the water?"

Helga turned to look at Ranger, too. Neither girl saw the huge wave growing behind them.

Ranger pawed at the stones and barked again, just as the wave broke and knocked Thora from her feet.

Helga whirled around when she heard the wave crash. Her cousin was gone.

"Thora!" She plunged into the water, diving headfirst into a breaking wave.

Ranger barked. Now Helga was gone, too. They were *both* in danger! Ranger pawed at the sand. How could he possibly find them in the wild, foaming waves?

Ranger looked up the path from the beach. There was no time to run for help. They were too far from the house. His only hope was to fight the ocean on his own.

Ranger turned back to the sea and plunged into the waves, just as Helga rose above the water. She had an arm wrapped around Thora as they splashed up onto the beach.

The girls collapsed on the smooth stones.

Ranger raced to their side and found them dripping, out of breath. And *laughing*.

"That was the biggest wave I've seen since the afternoon we first arrived," Helga said, brushing her dripping hair from her eyes. "That day, I was the one who got knocked over, remember? I owed you a rescue."

"Consider the debt paid," Thora said, hugging her cousin.

Funi trotted over and pounced on them. The girls laughed and pulled him into their circle. Then Helga reached out a hand to Ranger. "Here, dog. Everything's all right."

Ranger stepped up to Helga and let her scratch his wet head, but he kept a close eye on the rising waves. Soon, the girls stood up and Helga said, "We'd better take the eggs home."

She and Thora collected their sacks. They walked up the path together a ways, then said good-bye and set off toward their own family's longhouses.

Ranger and Funi walked with Helga. But Funi kept racing off on his own. Finally, Helga scooped him up and carried him under her arm. She reached down with her other hand and stroked Ranger's salty-wet head as they walked.

Ranger's heart had finally stopped pounding. But he missed Luke and Sadie. He missed his yard and home eggs and his dog bed in the mudroom. This strange, rocky place confused him. What was his job here supposed to be?

Helga didn't seem to need his help. She was better at rescuing than he was. How was he supposed to save someone who was so good at taking care of herself?

And if Ranger couldn't help, how would he find his way home?

Chapter 9

SPARKS IN THE SKY

Helga smiled all the way home. Her father had only been gone a day, but she was doing a fine job tending to things so far. She'd brought home more than enough eggs for the evening meal. How pleased Mother would be!

But when Helga pulled open the door to the longhouse, her mother was wailing.

"What's wrong?" Helga set the sack of eggs by the door and ran to her mother's sleeping bench. Mother sat hunched over with one hand on her bulging belly and the other on her lower back.

"The baby's coming sooner than we thought," Asa said. She stood beside Helga's mother, stroking her hair. Asa's face was worried, and Helga understood why. Her mother had lost babies before, when they were born too early. If it happened again, her father might never get his boy to help on the farm. Helga might never have a brother or sister of her own.

"Mother?" Helga said. "Can I do anything for you?"

Mother caught her breath and looked up at Helga. Her forehead glistened with sweat. Her eyes looked tired, but she tried to smile. "Not now. But soon, you will have a brother or sister."

Helga felt a jolt of excitement, but it turned to a nervous twist in her stomach when her mother cried out again. Helga looked up at Asa. "Father should be here."

Asa shook her head. "All is well. I brought my sister's children into the world back in Norway," she said. "Your mother is strong. Your father can meet the child when he returns. But I will need your help."

"Of course," Helga said. "I'll fetch water from the spring." She wasn't sure Asa needed water, but she didn't think she could stand to stay, listening to her mother cry in pain.

Helga was halfway to the cool spring near the lake when the ground rumbled again. Ranger and Funi, who'd been trotting along beside her, stopped and pricked up their ears. "Did you feel that?" Helga asked.

When the earth was steady under her feet again, Helga walked on to the spring and bent to fill her pail. Just as she finished, the sky grumbled. At first, Helga thought it was another storm, but the sky had been blue all day.

Then she looked up and gasped. A wall of sparks shot up from the earth, beyond the black rocks in the east. It looked as if the entire sky might catch fire. Helga had seen plumes of smoke before, when the earth rumbled and spit, but nothing like this. Nothing so big or so close.

She whirled to find Ranger and Funi. "Come! We must tell Asa and Mother."

Helga walked as quickly as she could without sloshing all the water from the pail. When she neared the longhouse, she could hear her mother's cries through the turf walls. Helga took a deep breath and went inside.

Asa looked up. "She is struggling. Wet a clean cloth for her forehead to cool her."

Helga did that while she described to Asa what she'd seen. "The very earth is spitting fire," she said, "and the ground is still rumbling."

Funi wandered off to sniff some bones in the refuse pile, but Ranger stayed close to Helga's side. He didn't like this trembling under his paws. It felt like the earth might tear open and swallow them all.

Asa left Helga's mother for a moment to look out the door. When she returned, her voice was urgent. "Your father must come home at once," she told Helga. "Your uncle will have to ride to the Althing and find him. Take Rosta to your uncle's farm and tell him that —"

"I can go myself," Helga said. She wanted to help her mother. She wanted the baby to be born safely. "I heard Father talking with Mother about the way he would go. I can ride it in less than a day."

"You mustn't go alone," Mother murmured. But she could barely keep her eyes open.

Asa looked at Helga and hesitated. "It would be faster . . ."

"Much faster. What if I ride all the way to my uncle's farm and no one is home?" Helga reached for her woolen sack. She took out the eggs and filled the bag with dried fish and mutton, grain, and a bladder for drinking. She would leave before there could be more discussion.

When Helga finished packing, she returned to her mother's bench. Asa was striking jasper and flint together to light a fish-oil lamp. The first sparks flew from the stone and disappeared, but then the twisted strands of cotton grass caught fire. The flame flickered on Mother's pale face, and she opened her eyes.

"I won't be gone long, Mother," Helga whispered. "Then Father will be here for you, too."

Her mother nodded weakly and reached out a hand. Helga squeezed it, then turned to go. She lifted her woolen bag over her shoulder, scooped Funi up from the rubbish pile, and tucked him into a sling against her over-dress. Ranger followed her to the door.

"Wait! The wind will be cold in the mountains. Take your father's heavier cloak." Asa wrapped the too-big cloak around Helga's shoulders, then bit her lip. "It makes you look so small," Asa said quietly. "You should wait until morning, at least."

"The days are long now, and the nights short. I won't have to travel far in darkness. And the sooner I go, the sooner I can return with Father," Helga said, and headed out the door.

She wished she felt as brave as her words.

Chapter 10

HELGA'S JOURNEY

The sun was still bright when Helga set out on Rosta. The old horse plodded along, and Ranger trotted beside it. Helga kept Funi snuggled in a sling at her side. There would be no time to chase him if he ran off. She'd thought about leaving him back at the long-house but worried he'd get into trouble. Funi might still be a pup, but if he went after the hens, Gunnarr would kill him without a thought.

Funi squirmed against Helga. She pulled him close as they came to the first water crossing. This river spilled down from the snowy mountains in little rocky cascades. Rosta hesitated on the bank, pawing the muddy earth.

The river was running fast from the recent rains, but it wasn't deep. Helga looked down at Ranger. "Are you ready to cross?"

Ranger followed Helga and Rosta toward the other bank. The river was wide but shallow. Ranger's paws sank into the silty bottom, but soon he climbed onto the far shore and shook himself dry.

They started off over the rocks again. Helga could already see another river, flowing like a dark ribbon over the land. When they approached the water's edge, she pulled on Rosta's reins. She wasn't ready to cross yet.

This river was bigger and faster. The light in the evening sky had faded to a hazy, purple-red glow, and Helga couldn't tell how deep the water was. She wished there were a way around.

Helga looked back from where they'd come just as a wall of orange sparks shot up from the earth. She had to keep going. She had to find Father and bring him home.

"Go on, Rosta." She urged the horse off the bank, into the rushing current. Cloudy water swirled around Rosta's legs. The horse stumbled once, halfway across. Helga clung to Rosta's mane until he caught his footing, continued on, and climbed up onto the bank. Helga breathed a sigh of relief. Funi yipped at her side.

"Oh! I'm sorry!" She loosened her grip on the little fox pup. "I didn't realize how tightly I was holding you. But we made it, didn't we?" Helga looked down, expecting to see the shaggy yellow dog beside Rosta.

But Ranger wasn't there. He was still on the far bank, pawing the dirt. Ranger breathed in the wet river air. He smelled mud and torn-up plants that had washed down from the hills. This water was powerful.

Ranger had done some of his search-and-rescue training near a rushing river like this. He'd walked along the bank with Luke and Dad, sniffing for a missing person. He'd ridden in the front of a boat, too, trying to catch scents rising up from the water.

But there was no boat here. The only way to cross was on his own.

Ranger jumped into the gushing water. It was colder than the icy water that streamed from the garden hose at home. In an instant, the water was up to Ranger's chin. He'd only taken a few steps when the current swept his paws out from under him.

Chapter 11

TO THE ALTHING

Ranger pawed and paddled, but the water carried him downstream as if he were another torn-up plant or tumbling stone. Rocks banged into his legs and sides as the water swept him along. Ranger barked. Helga shouted, but her words were lost in the water's roar.

Finally, the river grew wider, and the water slowed enough that Ranger was able to stand. The rocks were slippery, but he made his way to shore and followed the riverbank upstream to Helga.

"There you are!" She jumped down from Rosta and gave Ranger a big, soggy hug.

But there was no time to rest. The sky had turned from dusk to dark. A smoky, red moon rose over the hills, but soon, ash clouds from the eruption swallowed it up. Their only light came from the glow of spark showers in the east. Helga struggled to keep her eyes open as she rode Rosta through the darkness. She drifted off once but jerked awake when Funi started to slip from her arms.

All the while, Ranger walked beside Rosta. He still wasn't sure what his job might be. Helga didn't need help finding her way. She was better at crossing rivers than he was. Even Funi wasn't running off anymore. How was Ranger supposed to help? How would he ever get home?

When a sliver of dusty, rose-tinted light returned to the eastern sky, Helga stopped

Rosta at a river. Ranger lapped the cold water and shivered.

Helga dipped her hands into the water and took a long drink. She looked up at the smoky new light and sighed. There were no fluffy clouds to remind her of Sleipnir and Odin this morning, but Helga still thought of her grandfather when she looked up at the sky.

She hoped he was watching over her now. There was a long way to go, with another river to cross.

As they set out again, more and more ash fell from the sky. It clung to Helga's skin in the morning dampness. It matted in Ranger's fur and made him sneeze.

"Look." Helga squinted at something far up ahead. "That's the lake. We're close."

She urged Rosta to go faster, but this final part of their journey seemed to drag on forever.

Soon the rain started — a light mist, then a shower, then a pounding torrent. It churned up the earth along their path. Slippery, gritty mud seeped between Ranger's toes and scratched his paw pads.

Ranger didn't usually like baths, but he longed for one now. He wished Luke could soap him up, scrub the ash from his fur, and hug him dry with a soft towel.

Finally, the rain eased. Helga pointed to the lake. "Look!"

Birds flew along the shoreline. One rustled in the weeds, calling *swee-sweeeeeee!*

Ranger sniffed the damp air. He breathed in the smell of murky water and wildflowers that grew in the meadow nearby. He caught the scent of shore birds and horses and sheep.

And people. Hundreds and hundreds of people.

Chapter 12

CLIMBING HIGHER

Helga hurried Rosta along the shore. The buzz of men's voices rose over the cliffs near the lake. The tall stone walls made a perfect setting for the Althing. They bounced the Law Speaker's voice out over the rocks, so everyone could hear.

And there were so many people! Men rested on the flat rocks in groups of three or four, or gathered in larger, louder crowds by the lake. Besides the chieftains and their advisers, who sat on benches around the Law Speaker, hundreds of other men had come to take part in the gathering, perhaps to settle disputes like her father's.

Every open area around the lake and cliffs bustled with people.

Helga searched the sea of faces. Where was Father?

Helga tried to sit up taller, but her heart sank with despair. Searching for him in this enormous crowd was like trying to find a tiny piece of silver on a vast, pebbly beach. Helga stopped Rosta and climbed off. She patted Ranger on the head and looked up at the tall rock where the Law Speaker stood. When he spoke, everyone's eyes would be on him. Helga wished she could climb up beside the Law Speaker and look out over the crowd.

That was impossible. But perhaps if she found another high rock, she'd be able to spot her father's red beard.

The cliffs that towered over the Law Rock and the rest of the valley would be perfect. They were high but no steeper than the rocks Helga climbed to hunt eggs. She got back onto Rosta and led him through the mob to the base of the cliffs. Some of the men stared and whispered as she passed. She urged Rosta on so there would be no time for them to question why a young girl had come to the Althing.

Helga didn't stop until she reached the rocky ledges that towered above the assembly. Up close, they looked higher than the puffin cliffs. And more treacherous.

But then Helga spotted flowers growing out of the red-brown stones. The tiny purple and white blooms reminded her that she was a part of this land, too. She was strong and tough. She could find her father and bring him home.

Helga lowered her head and took off the sling she'd been wearing to carry Funi as they traveled. When she set it gently on the rocks, the little pup bounded out, jumped up, and swiped at Rosta's swishing tail.

"Be careful or you'll get kicked." Helga pulled Funi away from the old horse. Then she knelt until she was nose to nose with Ranger. "Stay with him. All right?" She pointed to Funi, then looked way up, toward the top of the tall rocks. She took off her cloak — it was too bulky for climbing — and arranged it on the ground to make a nest for Ranger and Funi. "You can rest on Father's cloak." She patted the thick wool and said once more, "Stay here. I'll be back soon." Then she turned to the rocks and looked for a place to climb.

A gentle slope led up one part of the cliff, but the rocks there were loose and crumbly.

They gave way every time Helga set foot on them. Instead, she chose a steeper grade with strong, solid rocks and began to climb.

At first, it was easy. There were wide ledges for her feet and clean, dry grips for her hands. About halfway up the cliff, a jagged rock caught the strap of Helga's overdress. Helga tugged herself free, but the brooch that held her strap tore away and plunged down the rock face. It clanged off the jagged stones and bounced over the rocks far below.

Helga's heart thudded in her chest as if it were trying to escape. She paused to catch her breath and tipped her head to look up. She'd made it halfway. Perhaps she was high enough already.

Carefully, Helga turned her head to look over the crowd. The Law Speaker started talking, and everyone pushed in to listen. Helga thought she caught a glimpse of her father, but another man stepped in front of him before she could be sure. She'd have to climb higher.

Helga took a deep breath and reached for another handhold. The rock felt a little loose, but it held. She found a crack for her foot, pushed herself up, and turned to look for her father.

But he was nowhere to be found. Helga sighed and found another tiny ledge for her foot. She pushed her hand into a crack high above her head, curled her fingers, and lifted herself to the new ledge.

Her foot only pressed down for an instant before the rock crumbled away beneath it. Helga lost her other foothold and cried out. She hung from the cliff by her hands as loose stones tumbled down and smashed onto the rocks below.

Helga searched the wall with her feet. She

pressed her fingers into the crack as hard as she could. Her arms burned, and the rough stone cut into her fingers, but she held on long enough to find another narrow ledge for one foot.

Helga pressed herself close to the rocks. Her heart thumped against the cliff, and the rough stone scratched her cheek. She didn't dare move her head to turn and look for her father. The tiniest move might send the rest of the rocks crumbling to the ground, and her along with them. Helga clung with both hands, trying to keep as much of her weight as possible off the ledge so it wouldn't break.

But her fingers and arms burned. She couldn't hold on much longer.

"Help!" Helga shouted into the rock. "Please help!"

Ranger barked from the base of the cliff. He pawed Funi over behind some rocks and hoped he'd stay. Then he sniffed at Helga's too-big cloak. It smelled like Rosta and Helga from the journey, but someone else, too. Helga's father.

Helga called out again, her voice tight with fear. Ranger knew he couldn't save her.

But he could find someone who would.

Chapter 13

RESCUE ON THE ROCKS

Ranger left Funi behind at the base of the cliff and raced toward the assembly. He could hear Helga calling, but none of the men seemed to notice.

Ranger made his way into the crowd and slowed down, sniffing for a trace of Helga's father.

This busy place was full of smells. There were horses and sheep, meat cooking and vegetables rotting. There were earthy smells — dirt and rock and lake — and people smells, too. Ranger climbed over boulders through the shadows. He searched the crowd until finally . . .

There!

Ranger picked up the smell from the too-big-for-Helga cloak. He kept his nose low and tracked the scent through the crowd. There were so many men talking and shouting. Some gathered around booths selling cooked meat or animal skins. Others wandered through the crowd begging for food or silver. None of them were Helga's father.

Ranger followed his scent to a spot sheltered from the wind, not far from the big ledge where a loud man was speaking.

And *there*! Helga's father was leaning against a rock. Ranger raced up to him and barked. At first, her father frowned and pushed Ranger out of the way. But Ranger jumped up and pawed at his chest. Father stumbled back and looked more closely. "You're the hound

Helga brought home." He looked around. "How did you come to be here?"

Ranger barked again. He nudged Helga's father in the direction of the cliffs. Ranger raced ahead, and circled back until her father picked up his sack from the ground and followed.

Ranger couldn't hear Helga shouting anymore. He ran faster. Had the tiny ledge that held her already crumbled and sent her falling to the rocks below?

When Ranger reached the base of the cliff, Helga was still holding on.

"Rosta?" Father stared at the horse tied to the rocks, confused.

Ranger looked up and barked. Finally, Helga's father looked up, too.

"Oh!" He sucked in his breath, then shouted, "Helga, hold on!" He tore through his sack, and pulled out a coil of walrus-skin rope like the one Helga had used on the puffin cliffs. Funi swiped at the rope, batting it around until Father pulled it away and ran to a ledge.

Father pulled himself up, step by crumbling step.

Hand. Hand.

Foot. Foot.

Reach again.

"Helga!" he called when he was at her level. "Don't move. I'll drop a rope to pull you up when I reach the top!"

As her father climbed higher, a ledge that held his left foot broke away. Rocks tumbled to the ground below and broke into pieces. Father strained to hold on while he scrambled and stretched to find another crack. Finally, he pressed both big hands onto the crumbling edge of the cliff and hoisted himself up.

"I am tying the rope around a boulder and

lowering the other end to you," he called down to Helga as he uncoiled it. It snaked down along the rocks. "Grab on! I'll pull you up!"

Helga heard her father's voice. She felt the rope brush the top of her head. But she couldn't grab it. Her fingers were numb, jammed into the crack. Her heart fluttered with fear. She couldn't move. "I can't!" Hot tears raced down her cheeks.

"Hold on!" Helga's father paced. Not far from where Helga was trapped was a ledge that stretched all the way to the top of the cliff. Her father lowered himself slowly, testing its strength, but before he had all his weight on it, a piece cracked off and smashed on the rocks below.

Ranger whined. He felt something scratch at his tail and turned to see Funi, batting at it like he'd swiped at Father's rope.

That was what Helga needed — someone to push the end of the rope to her!

Ranger looked up at the dusty, crumbly slope. Without thinking about whether it would hold his weight, he bounded up the rocks. He felt the loose ones shifting under his paws, but he didn't stop. He climbed all the way to the top of the slope, past Helga's father along the top of the cliff. Then he carefully stepped out onto the ledge that led to Helga.

Helga had closed her eyes to concentrate on not letting go, but when Ranger barked, she opened them and sucked in her breath. "How did you get up here?" she whispered.

Ranger inched farther along the narrow ledge until he could reach the rope that dangled from the top of the cliff. He stretched out a paw and batted it toward Helga.

It bumped against her arm.

Ranger barked. He batted the rope toward her, again and again.

Helga felt it brush her wrist. Her heart was beating so hard she feared it might set off another rockslide.

She gripped the rock tighter with her right hand while she wiggled the fingers of her left hand free. She could barely feel them, but the rope was thick and rough, and before Helga realized what she was doing, she had it tight in her hand.

"Grab it with both hands!" her father shouted. Helga looped the rope twice around her wrist so it would hold even if she couldn't. She pulled her other hand from the crevice and held on as her father pulled from above. Helga's elbows scraped against the rocks as she rose, inch by inch, to the top of the cliff. Her hands were raw, and every muscle in her body burned, but she was safe.

Carefully, Ranger climbed back up the ledge. He was waiting when Helga collapsed to the earth. Father dropped to his knees and held her.

"I had to come find you," Helga cried. "Mother is having the baby!"

"Already? Is she all right?" Father asked.

Helga blinked up at him through her tears. She remembered her mother's wails. She remembered Asa's worried eyes, the sparks and smoke pouring into the sky, and she whispered, "I don't know."

Chapter 14

DANGEROUS CROSSING

Ranger, Helga, and her father climbed down from the cliffs. As Helga walked toward Rosta, she stepped on something and looked down to find her brooch that had torn loose and fallen. The iron was scuffed and scarred, and the pin had snapped off. Helga shivered, remembering how the brooch had bounced off the jagged rocks.

She tucked the broken brooch into her sack. Then she looked at Ranger and bent to kiss the damp fur on his head. "Thank you," she whispered.

Helga and her father mounted their horses and rode away from the crowds, toward home. Helga carried Funi in the sling at her side again. Ranger trotted along beside them.

It was slower than the ride here. Rain still poured from the gray sky and puddled between rocks along the path. The horses plodded through the mud.

With every step, Helga's chest grew tighter with worry and impatience. Even with the long days of sunlight, they'd never make it home before night fell. She was thankful for the warmth of the fox pup. Father hadn't said a word when she'd scooped Funi up as she climbed back onto Rosta. She wasn't sure if he hadn't noticed or was too worried about her mother to care.

As they traveled south and east, the sky darkened. At first, Helga was puzzled that night was falling so early. Then she realized it was the clouds — full of not only rain, but soot from the fire that shot up from the earth. The streams they crossed were thick with ash. Wet, gray dust made the rocks slick as ice.

Ranger spread his toes to keep from skidding down the rocky bank of a creek. He'd learned to climb over slippery things in his search-and-rescue training with Luke and Dad. Luke had led him over all kinds of different surfaces — plastic tarps and plywood covered with aluminum foil. Ranger had practiced walking up and down metal ladders at different slants, and that training helped him to steady himself on the slick rocks. But training had never lasted this long. When would he get to go home?

The rain finally eased, but the sky was still dark with ashen clouds when they came to the last river crossing. Helga hesitated at the bank. She'd been skittish about crossing this deep, rocky water on the way to Thingvellir. Now the river was running higher and faster. She had to shout over the water to ask her father, "Is it safe to go on?"

Ranger sniffed along the bank. This wasn't where he and Helga had crossed before. The current was faster here, and Ranger couldn't tell how deep the water might be. He whimpered and pawed at the rocks.

Father hesitated, too. He sat up taller on his horse and looked to the far bank. Helga knew he was thinking of Mother when he nodded briskly. "It's the only way back," he said, and started to urge his horse into the racing current.

Ranger barked until Father stopped in the shallow water and looked back. Ranger raced along the bank of the river until he picked up Rosta's scent from before. It was faint and clouded by the rain and ash, but Ranger followed the scent trail down the river until he found the spot where they'd crossed. He barked again.

"Father, wait!" Helga cried. She guided Rosta over the rocks and looked at the river where Ranger had stopped. "It looks safer here — not as fast or deep."

Father backed his horse out of the water and followed Helga to the new spot downstream. The river was still treacherous, but they made their way across.

Ranger waited until they were safe on the far bank. He pawed the sooty mud. This river with its frothy current made his neck prickle.

But Ranger knew he had to cross. He jumped from the bank, and the water swept him up before his paws even touched the rocky bottom. Ranger heard Helga shout something over the river's gushing roar. He paddled as hard as he could, trying to hold his chin over the rushing water.

Finally, his paws found rocks and mud. Ranger braced himself against the current and pushed to the far bank. He climbed out onto the slippery rocks and shook himself. Helga was way upstream, but she'd waited for him.

Ranger made his way to her, and together, they caught up with her father.

The hills were scarred with landslides from the heavy rains. They rode through deeper and deeper ash as they approached the valley.

"It's just over this ridge," Father said. His voice was hopeful, but the worry lines around his eyes made Helga's heart race.

Mud and ash had already covered so much of the land. Would they arrive only to find the longhouse buried?

Chapter 15

SAYING HELLO . . .
SAYING GOOD-BYE

Helga held her breath as they crested the top of the ridge. When she looked out, she felt a rush of peace stronger than any river. There was the longhouse, safe and solid. Smoke rose from the roof and curled into the twilight sky.

"Thank the gods!" her father said, and started down the hill.

Helga and Ranger galloped after him, all the way to the longhouse. When her father opened the door, Helga heard a cry sweeter than anything in the world.

"She came through it well," Asa said from the fireplace as she stirred a pot of stew.

Helga's mother lay on her bench, nursing the new baby. She looked up at Helga and her father, and tears streamed down her face. "You're home," she whispered. She gave Father an exhausted smile and said, "Come meet your new daughter."

Father bent and kissed the baby. He turned to Helga. "Thank you," he said. "Your sister is so lucky to have you."

"Thank you, Father," Helga said. She hesitated, then whispered, "I thought you might be disappointed it's another girl."

Tears shone in her father's eyes. "How could I be anything but grateful to have another beautiful, brave daughter like you?"

Helga's heart warmed away all the chill from the rain and wind of their journey. She put Funi down, still wrapped in his sling, and knelt beside her mother's bench. When she reached out to touch her sister's hand, the baby wrapped her tiny fingers around Helga's. "She's strong," Helga said, and smiled. "She'll be good at climbing rocks with me someday."

Ranger stepped up beside Helga and sniffed the baby's head. Babies always smelled so good and new. Funi tried to jump on the bench, but Ranger gently pawed him down. Climbing on the new baby was a bad idea.

But Father had already noticed the fox pup. He frowned at Funi, then lifted his gaze to Helga. "I see you've brought us another visitor?"

Helga stood and scooped Funi into her arms. "He's a baby, Father. His mother is gone. You . . ." Helga hesitated. "I think she was the one that went after the hens."

Father's eyes softened. "I see. And you've decided to take her place."

"He's a good pup," Helga said. "Truly."

"Well, then." Father reached out and patted the fox pup in Helga's arms. "Perhaps he should stay with us until he's ready to hunt on his own."

Helga's face broke into a smile. "Thank you, Father!"

The baby started fussing then. Her hearty cry filled the longhouse. But over the cries, Ranger heard a quiet hum.

It came from under one of the benches. There, Ranger found his first aid kit, tucked among coiled rope and game pieces. He pawed it out from under the bench, took the leather strap in his teeth, and started for the longhouse door.

"What's that?" Helga called. "Where are you going?"

Ranger pawed at the door until Helga opened it. Curious, she followed him outside.

The air still smelled of ash, but the storm of fire had ended. No more billowing smoke. No more sparks. The sky was quiet and dark.

Ranger put the first aid kit down and trotted over to Helga. He jumped up on her and licked her face.

Helga laughed, then tipped her head. "Where are you going, dog?" She opened the longhouse door and held it. "Don't you want to come back inside?"

Ranger looked at the light from the fire and caught a scent of the stew bubbling over it. It smelled delicious, but he was ready to go home.

Ranger nuzzled Helga's hand. Then he turned and walked back to the old metal box, humming even louder now in the muddy ash.

"You can always come back if you want," Helga said quietly. But she had a feeling she might not see this shaggy golden dog again.

"Wait!" She ran inside and reached into her sack to find her brooch with the broken pin — the one she'd lost on the cliffs and found again. She ran to Ranger, knelt, and hugged him. "Here," she said, and tucked the metal brooch carefully under his collar. "You can keep this to remember me." Then she went back inside, to her parents and new sister.

Ranger nuzzled the strap of the old metal box around his neck. He could feel it growing warm at his throat. The humming got louder, and bright light spilled from the cracks in the box. *Too bright!* Finally, Ranger had to close his eyes.

When he opened them, Zeeshan and Noreen's new fur ball was sitting in Ranger's dog bed, wagging its tail.

Chapter 16

WHO'S SLEEPING IN MY BED?

Ranger barked. The puppy yipped back at him. Then Luke came running into the room. Sadie, Zeeshan, and Noreen piled in behind him.

"Poor Ranger," Luke said, laughing. "Is somebody trying to take over your bed?"

Ranger pawed at his blanket. The puppy pawed back and reminded Ranger of Funi, with its too-big paws and curious, blinking eyes. It was almost cute.

But it still didn't belong in his bed. Ranger barked again, and the pup jumped out and skittered back to Noreen.

"Your bath is ready upstairs, Ranger. We need to get you cleaned up before — hey, what's that?" Luke knelt down next to Ranger. He eased the metal brooch from under Ranger's collar and held it up to the light.

"What is it?" Sadie asked.

"Some fancy, old metal thing," Luke said. "Maybe he dug it up in Mom's garden." Luke patted Ranger's muddy fur.

Ranger took the brooch in his teeth and dropped it into his dog bed. He lowered his head until the first aid kit strap slid off. He pawed at his blanket until it covered them both.

Ranger sat down and breathed in the scent of the mudroom. He could smell Luke and Sadie's soccer shoes. Wet raincoats and visiting puppy. And from the kitchen: sweet, spicy spaghetti sauce bubbling on the stove.

"Get that dog cleaned up before we sit down for supper!" Mom called.

"Let's go, Ranger!" Luke gave Ranger a scratch behind the ear, and they raced up the back stairs.

The steamy bathroom air reminded Ranger of the hot pool in the rocks where he'd splashed with Helga. He'd done his work. She was home now, with her parents and her new baby sister. And Ranger was home, too.

"Come on, boy. Let's get this over with." Luke patted the tub with his hand. Ranger put his front paws up on the slippery edge, and Luke lifted him in. He poured warm water over Ranger's fur with a plastic cup, sudsed him up with dog shampoo, and poured water over him again to rinse it off.

Ranger shook himself and splashed some water on Luke. Luke laughed and gave Ranger a good scratch behind his ears. Ranger leaned into Luke's warm, soapy hand. He'd miss the brave, strong girl who climbed cliffs. And the warm water in the rocks had been fun.

But there was no better place for a bath than home.

AUTHOR'S NOTE

Often, when we picture Vikings, we imagine fierce men who ravaged coastal villages in the eighth century. This image of Vikings is true enough; ships did indeed leave Norway to raid English towns and monasteries, stealing and even taking people captive as slaves or holding them for ransom. But the Viking Era was also a time of migration. Families like Helga's left Norway not to raid, but to settle on a new island with more farmland.

That island is now the country of Iceland, where I spent a week doing research for

Ranger's latest adventure. I had the opportunity to explore the same glaciers that Helga would have seen as her ship neared Iceland's shore . . .

. . . and to enjoy some of Iceland's natural hot springs like the one where Helga and Ranger clean up after their day on the cliffs.

The same geothermal activity that creates Iceland's wonderful, warm pools for bathing also leads to eruptions like the one Helga's family lives through in this story. Historians know about that event — the eruption of Mount Eldgjá in 934 AD — from the tephra layers that tell Iceland's geological stories.

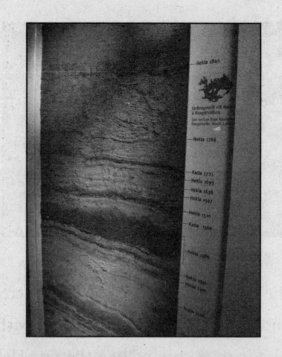

Hekla 1845

Jarðvegssnið við Næfurholt
á Rangárvöllum.
Soil section from Næfurholt,
Rangárvellir, South Iceland.

Hekla 1766

Katla 1721
Hekla 1693
Hekla 1636
Hekla 1597

Hekla 1510
Katla 1500

Hekla 1389

Hekla 1341
Hekla 1300

Hekla 1104

Hekla 1104

Eldgjá ~934

Landnámslag ~870
Settlement Tephra Layer

Because of these historic eruptions, much of Iceland's landscape remains stark and rocky. Hardening lava has formed fascinating tunnels and caves like the one where Helga takes shelter early in the story.

It was near one of those caves that I met the arctic fox pup that provided the inspiration for Funi. This pup, like Helga's, had taken to hanging around people after its mother was killed. It was a frequent visitor to the base camp near Thrihnukagigur Volcano.

Puffins are also native to Iceland. Hunting and gathering eggs from these birds provided food for the island's early settlers. Today, Iceland is the only country in the world that still allows puffin hunting (during a short season each April), a practice that's grown more controversial as the numbers of puffins have diminished worldwide. I saw puffin on the menu at a number of restaurants in Reykjavík but was not interested in trying it. I much preferred to watch these charming, orange-footed birds fly in and out of their nests on the ocean cliffs and spent hours doing that one evening in Dyrhólaey, on Iceland's southern coast.

Helga's journey to find her father is one that many of Iceland's early settlers made. The Althing is the world's oldest still-existing parliament. It was established in 930 AD by chieftains who realized that, in the absence of a king, their new land needed a way to make laws, maintain order, and talk about issues that affected the whole island. So for two weeks each summer, they gathered at Thingvellir, a beautiful, rugged place beside a lake, where great stone cliffs create a sort of amphitheater. The Law Speaker would recite the island's laws from the Law Rock in the shadow of the great cliffs while hundreds of people listened. Today, the area is every bit as stunning and often just as crowded, though its modern visitors tend to arrive on tour buses instead of horses.

Helga's way of life — and the island of Iceland as a whole — changed significantly when the country adopted Christianity around 1000 AD. The country was divided into parishes, and people were taxed for the first time. Power shifted to the church, and though it was decided that people could still practice their old pagan religion in private, many ended up persecuted as a result.

Before this shift, Helga's people didn't have a written language, other than the symbols called runes that people sometimes carved into rock, wood, and bone. But with Christianity came the Latin alphabet, and around the twelfth century, Icelanders began using it to tell the stories of their ancestors in colorful detail. These sagas, which talk about real historical people but also touch on magic and mythology, are looked upon as a mix of history and folklore. Historians are always interested in new archaeological discoveries in Iceland, to see where the artifacts can confirm the details of the saga. They were excited when an archaeological dig in Reykjavík during the 1970s revealed the remains of a longhouse, right where the sagas say Iceland's first settler built his farm. That site is a museum now, showing not only the longhouse remains but also artifacts from the island's first settlers. Among them are fragments of the brooches that women often wore, like the one Helga gives Ranger when she says good-bye.

FURTHER READING

In the case of Iceland's early settlers, history is what we find at the intersection of story and archaeology. I relied on both in researching Helga's story. If you'd like to learn more about her world, and about search-and-rescue dogs like Ranger, check out the following books and website:

D'Aulaires' Book of Norse Myths by Ingri d'Aulaire and Edgar Parin d'Aulaire. (New York Review Children's Collection, 2005)

"Sagas Portray Iceland's Viking History" by Stefan Lovgren http://news.nationalgeographic.com /news/2004/05/0507_040507_icelandsagas .html

Sniffer Dogs: How Dogs (and Their Noses) Save the

World by Nancy Castaldo (Houghton Mifflin Harcourt, 2014)

Viking (DK Eyewitness Books) by Susan Margeson (DK Publishing, 2005)

SOURCES

I am most grateful to the staff of The Settlement Exhibition Reykjavík 871±2, the National Museum of Iceland, and Vikingaheimar (Viking World), not only for the excellent research and archaeology behind their exhibits but also for answering my many questions about Helga's world and culture.

Many thanks to the Champlain Valley K-9 Search and Rescue Unit, particularly Shannon Bresett, Kelly Gidman, and their dogs, Oakland and Easton, for helping me to learn how these amazing canine rescuers do their work.

The following resources were also especially helpful:

American Rescue Dog Association. *Search and Rescue Dogs: Training the K-9 Hero*. Hoboken, NJ: Wiley Publishing, 2002.

Brown, Nancy Marie. *The Far Traveler: Voyages of a Viking Woman*. New York: Harcourt, 2007.

Brown, Nancy Marie. *Song of the Vikings: Snorri and the Making of Norse Myths*. New York: Palgrave Macmillan, 2012.

Bulanda, Susan. *Ready! Training the Search and Rescue Dog*. Freehold, NJ: Kennel Club Books, 2010.

Byock, Jesse L. *Viking Age Iceland*. New York: Penguin Books, 2001.

Short, William R. *Icelanders in the Viking Age: The*

People of the Sagas. Jefferson, NC: McFarland &
Company, 2010.

Sverrisdottir, Bryndis, Ed. *Reykjavík 871±2
Landnámssýningin The Settlement Exhibition.*
Reykjavík: Reykjavík City Museum, 2006.

ABOUT THE AUTHOR

Kate Messner is the author of *The Seventh Wish*; *All the Answers*; *The Brilliant Fall of Gianna Z.*, recipient of the E. B. White Read Aloud Award for Older Readers; *Capture the Flag*, a Crystal Kite Award winner; *Over and Under the Snow*, a *New York Times* Notable Children's Book; and the Ranger in Time and Marty McGuire chapter book series. A former middle-school English teacher, Kate lives on Lake Champlain with her family and loves reading, walking in the woods, and traveling. Visit her online at www.katemessner.com.

Ranger travels to San Francisco and meets Lily Chen. When the Great Earthquake hits, Ranger helps Lily flee the collapsing mission house she lives in. Then they help another girl, May Wong, save her brother from fallen rubble. Ranger and his new friends try to make their way through the ruined city, but can they escape crumbling buildings and racing fires, all while facing anti-Chinese discrimination? Turn the page for a sneak peek!

Chapter 1

MORNING OF THE EARTH DRAGON

At first, Lily Chen thought it was another nightmare. The roaring sea. The slamming waves. So often, her dreams took her back to the crowded, lurching ship that had brought her across the ocean to San Francisco five years ago.

But this nightmare didn't end when Lily opened her eyes.

An angry roar shook the mission home where she lived with fifty other girls and women. Lily sat up in bed as the mirror over the dresser crashed to the floor. It smashed into shining pieces that danced and skidded over the wood. The whole house rocked as if an angry giant shook it in his palm. The window rattled itself free and crashed to the street below.

Lily's bed jumped up and down and sideways until she was thrown to the floor. She crawled to the open window and pulled herself up to look outside. The street was a rolling wave of cobblestones.

People stood in their nightshirts, looking up to the sky. An old man raced into the street in his bare feet, shouting, "Aiyaaa, dei lung zan! Aiyaaa, dei lung zan!" which means "The earth dragon is wiggling!"

Lily understood this was one of California's earthquakes. Usually, they were trembles that shook pictures from the walls. But today, Lily felt like one of the rats that the neighborhood dogs liked to catch and thrash about. She staggered back to her bed and clung to the headboard.

The house swayed like a ferryboat in a storm. Ceiling timbers groaned. Chimney bricks crashed onto the roof. Lily's room filled with dust as the plaster walls cracked and crumbled.

It felt as if the shaking might never end, but finally the house settled. Lily picked her way through the broken mirror pieces to the door.

It was jammed shut, stuck in the twisted door frame. But Lily was big for her age, and strong. As a servant, she'd lugged pails of stew and heavy baskets of vegetables through Chinatown every day. She yanked until the frame let go and sent her flying backward across the glass-strewn floor.

"Are you all right?" a voice called from the hallway. It was Donaldina Cameron, the woman who ran the mission house. The girls called her Lo Mo, or "old mother," but she was nothing like the mother Lily remembered from home. Lily's real mother smelled of earth from working the farm. Her real mother was far away over the ocean, in China's Guangdong province.

Lo Mo's mission house was better than being beaten as a servant, but it was a long way from home.

"We've been shaken, but this good house is still standing," Lo Mo told the girls. "Come downstairs, and we'll see about breakfast."

Lily and the other girls climbed over fallen bookshelves and got themselves dressed. The quake had rattled pictures from the walls and toppled dressers, but somehow the fishbowl on the little hallway table had survived.

"Gum Gum!" Lily rushed over, knelt down, and smiled at the little fish. Some of his water had sloshed out onto the table, but he was all right. "Your golden color certainly brought you good fortune this morning," she said.

When Lily went downstairs, her heart sank. The girls had cleaned the house spotless that week. They'd swept and dusted and draped a beautiful fishnet in the chapel room to get ready for the annual meeting of the people who ran the home. Now all the dishes had been tossed about and broken. The chimney had collapsed. How would they even cook?

But Lo Mo settled everyone down, and soon there was breakfast. Someone brought baskets of bread from a bakery nearby. Another neighbor appeared with apples and a kettle of tea. Lily sat down with the others at the little white tables and recited a Psalm from the Bible.

"The Lord is my Shepherd; I shall not want . . ."

Lily's mind wandered. Even as the girls ate, there was talk of packing and going to the

Presbyterian church on Van Ness Avenue until it was certain the home would be safe.

Lo Mo told them to gather just a few things. They finished eating and set to packing up bundles of bedding, clothes, and a little food.

Outside, Chinatown buzzed with noise. Doors slammed. Voices filled with worry and fear drifted through the broken windows. When Lily returned to the kitchen and looked out the door, she understood why.

The sky was full of dust clouds where buildings had collapsed. In the distance, half a dozen dark plumes of smoke rose into the quiet sky.

The earthquake was only the beginning.

MEET RANGER

A time–traveling golden retriever with search-and-rescue training . . . and a nose for danger!